THE FAST LITTLE FOX
Jill Horton

Happy reading!
— Jill Horton

Copyright 2021 Jill Horton

All Rights Reserved. No part of this publication may be reproduced, distributed, or transmitted in any form or by any means, including photoshopping, recording, or other electronic or mechanical methods without prior written permission of the author and publisher, except in the case of the brief quotations embodied in reviews and certain other noncommercial uses permitted by copyright law. For information regarding permission, email the author at jill.horton.author@gmail.com.

This book is a work of fiction. Names, characters, and incidents, are either the product of the author's imagination or are used fictitiously, and any resemblance to actual persons living or dead, business establishment, events, or locales, is entirely coincidental.

ISBN: 978-0-578-32029-8 (paperback)
ISBN: xxx-x-xxxxxxx-x-x (hardcover)

First Edition Book, August 2021

Book cover design, illustration, editing, and interior layout by:

www.1000storybooks.com

DEDICATION

Thank you to my family, friends, and readers!
This book is dedicated to you.

Freddy Fox loved to have fun and go on new adventures. Today, he wanted to play in the forest.

"Don't run too fast!" his sister, Fiona, cautioned. "You might go too far by accident and get lost!"

"I am Fearless Freddy!" he replied. "Nothing scares me!"

Freddy whizzed past the kitchen and down the hall.

"Be home in time for supper!" Mama Fox called as he dashed out the door.

The fast little fox couldn't wait to do things he had never done before.

Once outside, Freddy made a beeline down the path that led toward the forest.

"That wooden fence isn't going to get in my way!" he thought with a grin.

With a mighty leap, Freddy dove over the boards. His tiny paws sank into the mud puddle waiting on the other side. Each paw squished and squashed as Freddy sloshed his way out of the goo. Once free, he zoomed past the neighbor's house and nearly ran right into Skipper Skunk.

"Slow down!" Skipper cried as Freddy sailed on by. "You left muddy paw prints all over my yard!"

Did Freddy listen? *No!* The fast little fox had places to go.

Freddy hopped and skipped along, chasing butterflies and blowing on dandelions as he went. At the bottom of a hill, three ducks swam together in a sparkling blue pond. Dolly Duck was the first to spot Freddy as he sped over the peak of the hill. Dorsey Duck and Dillon Duck stared with wide eyes at the flash of red fur getting closer and closer.

"Stop!" Dolly cried. "You're going to run right into the pond!"

The trio flapped and quacked to get his attention, but Freddy didn't slow down, and he didn't stop. The fast little fox fell into the pond with a loud *KERPLOP!*

Freddy swam back to shore while the ducks looked on, shaking their heads. The fox's coat was soggy and heavy as he stepped onto the sand. The duck siblings were shocked that Freddy didn't seem to mind the mess he was in—in fact, he was giggling at himself!

Droplets went flying into the air as Freddy wriggled the water away. The fast little fox planned to play all day.

Further in the forest, Beatrice Bear was nibbling berries for breakfast. She loved to savor the delicious morsels on her morning walk through the woods. Little did she know that her meal was about to be interrupted by Freddy the Fox, zooming by with lightning-quick speed.

With a *WHOOSH* of air, Beatrice's berries went flying everywhere.

"My breakfast!" Beatrice bellowed. She covered her eyes with her paws, barely believing what had just happened.

Freddy's stomach growled, and the sweet fruit looked yummy. The fast little fox snatched some up to fill his grumbling tummy.

"Maybe I can find something new to do up ahead!" Freddy said to himself excitedly.

He hurried forward, zigging and zagging here and there. Freddy was having such a good time speeding along that he didn't notice the changes in his surroundings right away...but after a while, the flowers didn't smell familiar, and the trees looked too tall. A canopy of thick green leaves hid the sky, and everything was quiet and still.

He had never been this deep in the forest before. The fast little fox didn't want to run anymore.

Nothing looked familiar, and he wasn't sure which way was home. Freddy sniffled and whimpered.

"What should I do?" Freddy asked aloud with a shaky sigh.

His shoulders slumped, and his tail trailed low to the ground. Just when he was about to give up, a friend appeared in a nearby tree. Reno Ringtail scampered down the tall trunk, and joined Freddy on an enormous rock.

"Do you need help? I can walk you back home," Reno offered his friend.

Freddy nodded and wiped his eyes. The fast little fox hadn't been very wise.

The two companions went off in the direction of the fox family's cozy den on the other side of the forest. Freddy filled Reno in on the events of his day while Reno listened quietly.

"Sounds like you were going so fast you didn't listen to others," Reno said. "That's why you got lost. I bet it hurt your friends' feelings, too."

Freddy nodded, feeling a little foolish. "That's true. How can I make it up to them?"

The ring-tailed cat helped his fox friend come up with a plan that everyone was sure to love.

They started by picking a fresh batch of berries for Beatrice the Bear. Freddy plucked the first few too fast, smooshing them and getting juice everywhere. So he tried again, slowly, and beamed with pride as the next berry stayed whole.

"I'm sorry for eating your berries, Beatrice," Freddy said, carefully placing the juicy treats on her porch. "I was going so fast I wasn't thinking straight."

The bear gave him a big hug and a warm smile. "I forgive you, little Freddy. Thanks for picking new berries for me!"

Freddy gave Beatrice a big huge smile. The fast little fox hadn't felt this good in a while.

As they passed by the pond, Freddy stopped in his tracks.

"Thank you for trying to warn me that I was getting too close to the water, earlier!" he called to the ducks as they waddled along.

Dolly, Dorsey, and Dillon greeted the fox and the ring-tailed cat with a loud cheer in return. "We're just glad you're okay!" the trio called. "Tomorrow, you two should come back and play with us, instead of just running by so quickly!"

Three new friends who wanted to play! The fast little fox happily exclaimed, "Okay!"

Next, Freddy and Reno visited Skipper Skunk. Together, they cleaned up the muddy paw prints Freddy had left behind that morning. Skipper thanked them for making up for his mistake.

Once the work was done, the two young friends sat down and listened to Skipper's stories. The skunk wove tales of pirates, dragons, and treasure.

Freddy used to think sitting still for so long would be a bore, but the fast little fox had more fun than he could ever ask for!

Finally, Freddy made it back home. He thanked Reno with a big hug for helping him find his way.

The delicious smell of freshly baked bread greeted the friends as Freddy opened the door. They found Papa, Mama, and Fiona playing a game together in the living room.

"Can Reno please stay for supper?" Freddy pleaded.

"Yes! Of course," Mama Fox answered with a broad grin. "Wash your paws first!"

Reno was happy to have made a good friend, while the fast little fox was thankful to be with his family again.

When all the food was ready to eat, everyone gathered around the table. The foxes and the ring-tailed cat chatted and laughed as they ate. Once the family and their guest finished their meal, Freddy's sister Fiona brought out a chocolate cake, and Freddy offered to pour everyone a tall glass of milk.

To his mother's surprise, he moved slowly and he didn't spill a drop. Was her fast little fox growing up?

Later that evening, the ring-tailed cat was ready to go back to his own home in the forest.

"Thank you for showing me how to get to my den, Reno! It was kind of you to help me!" Freddy said.

"You're welcome!" Reno replied. The fast little fox was grateful to have such a good friend by his side.

As Freddy was brushing his teeth before bed, a thought popped into his head. He still had something he needed to say to his sister.

"Fiona, you were right! I wandered too far away from home. I was running very fast and got lost," he admitted.

She smiled and said, "Freddy, it's okay. It happens to everyone! But now you know what to do if you make a mistake."

The fast little fox had learned and had fun. Freddy realized his best adventures had only just begun.

About the Author

Jill Horton loves creating magical worlds for children to learn in and explore. She and her husband have four kids who also love the adventures found in good books. One dog, two cats, and four parakeets joined the family's fun and literary travels. Now, Jill is inviting you to pick up one of her books and start your own family's storytime traditions too!

Made in the USA
Middletown, DE
30 April 2023